D1641129

下流

HOMEBOUND
KC Kwan

"Creatures erased by daylight can be found again in the darkness of night."
「在夜裡找回被陽光刪除的人事物。」
– Gu Zheng　顧錚

For my mother

## Foreword

KC Kwan's story is one of an insider. He didn't have the privilege to enjoy an expensive education, not even an amateur photography course. Kwan comes from a humble background. He has never known his father. His mum, a hawker, died when he was four, leaving him and his twin brother behind. He struggled at school and started working at the age of 18 at a printing company, an industry he is still involved with today.

About three years ago, he bought his first camera, a Nikon D3100. For the first time it was cheap enough for him. After reading his first book on photography, a free copy he grabbed from his printing company, he started, like most people, with shooting flowers and landscapes. However, he found it very boring and the book ended in the bin. He didn't like hiking anyway.

Looking for more inspiration, he turned to the World Wide Web and discovered artists such as Henri Cartier-Bresson and Robert Frank. However, he wasn't very fond of their straight and formalist style. Garry Winogrand was the first photographer that inspired him. There was something about his loose style, tilted frames and fascination for public life. But it wasn't until he bumped into a grainy black and white picture of a dog by Daido Moriyama that something struck a chord. He was drawn to the peculiar Japanese language that was so unlike its European or American counterparts, presenting a certain randomness that didn't stick to formal rules, but resonated with Kwan.

So a year later, he dumped his big camera (which tended to frighten his subjects anyway) and exchanged it for a smaller point-and-shoot Ricoh GXR. This was when KC Kwan started taking the night shots. Kwan's normal shifts are from 9pm to 6am, but sometimes he gets lucky and can leave earlier. After leaving the factory in Chai Wan, he normally takes the N118 bus to Sham Shui Po, has supper in Mong Kok and then wanders the streets for hours looking for old neighbourhoods. Since a night bus is a few dollars more expensive than the day one, he started out photographing just to kill time, until the first daytime bus operates again. This habit quickly grew to an obsession.

For these night shots, photographers normally go out in groups but he prefers to work solo. He endured strange encounters and was once attacked by a mad man who scratched his face like a wild cat. But when being asked if he ever fears the dark of night, he just shrugs his shoulders and replies a dry 'no'. What makes him uncomfortable is not shooting for a few days. By now photography is part of him and the one thing in life that gives him some dignity. 'In Hong Kong, if you have no degree, you are nothing.' he says. 'Photography is a way to experience and see the cruel world. Cruelty is part of this world and our lives.'

However KC Kwan doesn't want to be seen as a victim. 'I have a poor life but I'm happy.' When being asked about his dreams and ambitions, he stared and replied, 'I'm a "dried salted fish".' In Cantonese that's a metaphor for someone who has no dreams, ambitions or concrete plans. 'I just feel like I'm chasing something although I don't know what that something is.'

There are many people with cameras, but very few are photographers. Photography is about the way you feel the world. KC Kwan is a true gem capturing Hong Kong's dark underbelly, not as an observer but as an insider. He is just a normal guy, like so many quiet workers in Hong Kong enduring the hardship of life. However, Kwan has a special talent, a pure and genuine eye, which we were so lucky to discover and share with you.

Sarah Greene
Hong Kong, July 2013

# 前言

關錦昌的故事鮮為人知。他出身草根家庭，父親與他素未謀面；做小販的母親在他四歲時去世，只留下他與孿生弟弟相依為命。關未曾接受高等教育，攝影對他來說更是奢侈的嗜好。十八歲時，他毅然輟學並開始在印刷公司工作。

三年前，關錦昌開始自學攝影，並買了人生中第一部相機 Nikon D3100。由於經濟條件所限，關沒有能力負擔昂貴的器材，甚至他讀的第一本攝影書也只是從工作的印刷廠免費攫取。像大多數攝影新手一樣，他常練習拍攝風景及植物，但欠缺動感的題材很快就令他生厭，初期的作品他都不大滿意，就連攝影書最後也被他扔掉。

為取得拍攝靈感，關錦昌開始在網上欣賞其他攝影師的作品。Henri Cartier-Bresson 和 Robert Frank 整齊及注重形式的風格不引起關興趣；Garry Winogrand 的作品構圖鬆散，題材圍繞尋常大眾生活，卻令他著迷。森山大道一幀以狗作題材的黑白照片更深深震撼關的心靈，他欣賞森山大道的攝影風格，更由衷敬佩森山大道的攝影哲學，關發現攝影沒有一定的規則和方法，率性隨意的表達手法也能拍攝出好作品。

之後，他放下單反（事實上，體積龐大的相機也常常驚動他的拍攝對象），改用輕巧方便的 Ricoh GXR 趁晚間閒逛拍攝。關錦昌在柴灣某印刷廠返通宵更，偶爾幸運可提早下班，他會乘搭 N118 號巴士到深水埗，在旺角吃過飯後，他愛穿梭大街小巷，觀察舊區建築。起初，拍攝夜晚的街頭純粹是消磨時間的方法，因為通宵巴士的車費較貴，他通常等待至早上才乘車回家。但慢慢地，攝影已變成了他的習慣，甚至是生命中不可或缺的一部分。

街頭攝影師在晚上拍攝時通常三五成群，關錦昌卻偏愛在黑夜中獨自遊走，隨心尋找拍攝題材。獨來獨往有時也為他帶來麻煩，例如有一次，他在拍攝途中被一名神經失常的男子襲擊，抓傷了面部。當問到他會否因此害怕在晚間外出拍攝時，他聳肩說：「更令我感到不安的，是幾天沒有拍照。」對他而言，攝影除了是生活一部分，更是他的尊嚴。「在香港，沒有大學學位，你就甚麼都不是，」他說「現實是殘酷的，攝影讓我們看清楚殘酷的世界。」

然而，關錦昌不願被視作悲劇人物。「雖然窮，但我活得很快樂。」關自嘲自己是一條「鹹魚」。（在廣東俗語，「鹹魚」意指生活漫無目的、沒有理想、欠缺計劃的人。）「我正在追趕某些東西，雖然我並不清楚自己確實想追求甚麼。」

《下流》是關錦昌的首本攝影集，攝影師的鏡頭帶領你一同深入繁華鬧市的陰暗一隅。夜幕低垂，在柴灣登上巴士，沿途看見旺角一帶熱鬧的橫街窄巷和攤檔，停下來在簡陋齷齪的大牌檔享用地道的食物，窺視妓女與癮君子不足為外人道的生活。當夜行動物也停止活動，喧鬧的黑夜城被一片沉寂憂鬱的氣氛包圍。最後，晨曦的曙光打破寂靜，都市回復繁盛。

今天，相機不再是奢侈品，但真正稱得上攝影師的人卻不多。很多人窮畢生精力追求更先進的器材和純熟的技巧，然而攝影的本質是人與世界的聯繫。透過鏡頭，攝影師記錄低下階層在逼迫中掙扎，敘述出香港不為人知的黑暗一面。關錦昌並非置身事外的旁觀者，卻是黑夜城其中一個齒輪。他平凡而不起眼，就像其他同樣在生活的漩渦中奮力求存的普通人，每天營營役役為生計奔馳；同時他又與眾不同，憑著攝影的天賦和敏銳的觀察力，帶著相機走過一條又一條的街道，利用影像向觀眾述說一個又一個黑夜城的故事。

Sarah Greene

香港，二零一三年七月

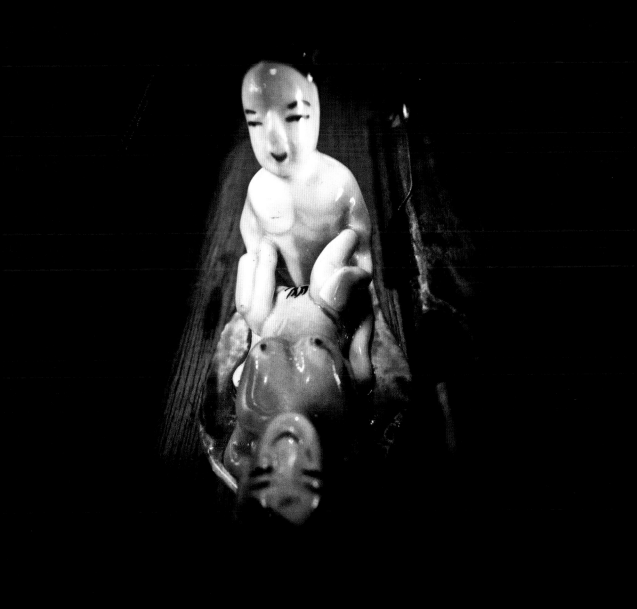

時段

10:00 ~ 13:00

13:00 ~ 16:00

16:00 ~ 19:00

19:00 ~ 22:00

22:00 ~ 01:00

01:00 ~ 04:00

04:00 ~ 07:00

07:00 ~ 10:00

-the first-
# JUNK STORY

**21/4/2012 07:30pm**

Fare: 票價 **$100(WALK IN ONLY)**

-Hidden agenda-

2A, Wing Fu Industrial Bldg, 15-17 Tai Yip Street,
Ngau Tau Kok, Kwun Tong, Hong Kong

香港牛頭角大業街15-17號永富工業大廈2樓A室

Performing:
演出單位：

Mesmerist
The3Think
AMS
Psyc´Lover
ParanoiD

Organizing party:
主辦單位　Junk MUSIC

Supreme

優質寫字樓
250'- 500'

寫字樓/倉

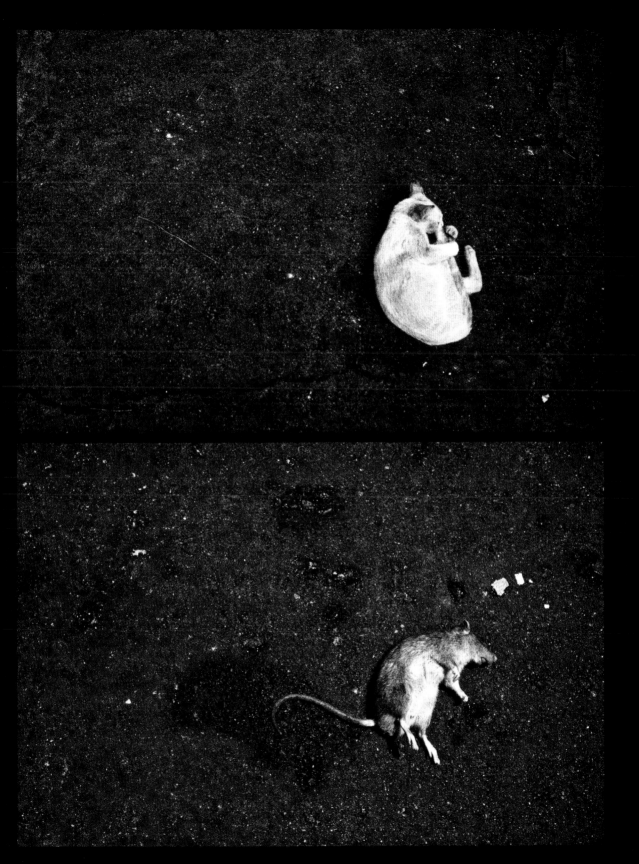

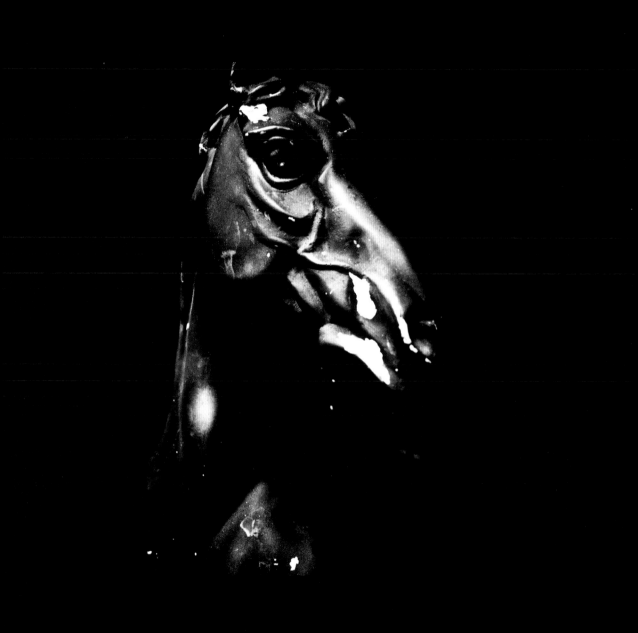